Karel van de Woestijne

THE DYING PEASANT

Translated and with an Introduction by
Paul Vincent

THE DYING PEASANT

KAREL VAN DE WOESTIJNE (1878-1929) was perhaps the greatest early twentieth-century Flemish poet. Heavily influenced by French symbolism, he wrote numerous volumes of verse, as well as short stories and a novel. Today he is most remembered for his novella *The Dying Peasant*, which was first published in 1918, and which is a classic of Flemish literature.

PAUL VINCENT studied at Cambridge and Amsterdam, and after teaching Dutch at the University of London for over twenty years became a full-time translator in 1989. Since then he has published a wide variety of translated poetry, non-fiction and fiction, including work by Achterberg, Claus, Couperus, Elsschot, Jellema, Mulisch, De Moor and Van den Brink. He is a member of the Society of Dutch Literature in Leiden, and has won the Reid Prize for poetry translation, the Vondel Prize for Dutch-English translation and (jointly) the Oxford-Weidenfeld Prize.

Contents

Introduction

KAREL VAN DE WOESTIJNE (1878-1929) was first and foremost a poet. Though he produced a good deal of journalism, literary criticism, shorter fiction and even a novel composed jointly with Herman Teirlinck, it was his thirteen volumes of poetry that represented his highest literary aspiration.

Born in Ghent, Van de Woestijne took a conscious decision to write in his native Dutch, unlike his contemporaries Emile Verhaeren (1855-1916) and Maurice Maeterlinck (1862-1949), who opted for the culturally more prestigious French language. Between 1900 and 1906 he spent two periods at an artists' colony in the village of Sint-Martens-Latem. He became the Belgian correspondent of several Dutch newspapers, and in 1920 was appointed to a professorship at Ghent University.

Van de Woestijne's early poetry is heavily influenced by such French decadent symbolists as Baudelaire, Laforgue, Barbey d'Aurevilly and Moréas. In the last three collections published in his lifetime (possibly conceived as a trilogy), there is an attempt to move beyond the senses to a mystical freedom of the spirit. One poem, much anthologised, from his last collection, can serve as an illustration of his vision of the constraints on the writer and expresses his decadent sensibility literally in a nutshell.

I am the hazelnut.—A worm soft and pale
lives in my chamber, gnaws me and is blind.
I am one whose seed makes darkness hale.
I'm emptiness that's never asked or whined.

I quit myself, myself on airy harming I impale.
I am the constant meal, enjoyed in a closed ring
of a worm dumb, impatient, thankless, pale.
But if a child's finger touches me, can guess my tale:
it hears my hollowness; I sound; I sing.

Given his lifelong devotion to poetry, it may seem ironic that the work by which Van de Woestijne is mainly remembered today should be the dialect tale of an old peasant visited on his deathbed by a succession of figures representing his five senses, reminding him of the joys of his modest existence.

But the literary historian Gerard Knuvelder sees this as a life 'totally dominated by the senses' and hence a reflection of writer's own problematic view of sensuality.[1]

—Paul Vincent

1 Gerard Knuvelder, *Handboek tot de geschiedenis der Nederlandse letterkunde,* vol. 4, 's-Hertogenbosch, 1961, p. 401.

THE DYING PEASANT

A N OLD peasant lay dying. His bed stood in
the upstairs room, in the sour-smelling air.
Dusk was falling and the peasant lay peering out
from the depths of his straw mattress, under the
blanket that was grubby and grey. His dark bony
fingers caught at the blanket, and he noticed it
for a second, and thought: 'See, I'm already ty-
ing up my bundle.' But he peered, with the flat
glazed sheen of his eyes above the taut yellow skin
of his cheekbones, and nothing moved across his
forehead or around his black sunken mouth. He
saw the tall bed, and behind it his yellow chest
with the Virgin Mary and the bowls on it. The
walls were stained blue with salt and the red
floor tiles were damp at the corners. He had long
been without a wife and his children had all left
home. Now an old woman came in occasionally.

He thought of her, when he looked at the chest and then at the chair. 'The chair's not straight,' he thought. He saw that the evening light lay in ridges across the rush seat of the chair. Then he felt a little cold around his shoulder. Where had the woman got to? He did not make any effort to get deeper under the blanket. He knew he was on his deathbed.

The evening grew greyer and greyer. Soon there was not even a glimmer of light on the porcelain holy water font. He saw that too. He saw next to it the print of Bertha's first communion. It still shone. What did it say on that print again? He searched for a while in his head. All he knew was: his Bertha had eleven children of her own now. There was his Domien too, but he was in America. Though he was married to a girl from the village. Her name was Felicita. She stood by his bedside: 'How are you, father?'—'Well,' he replied, 'a bit better than being possessed by the devil.' That was difficult to say: his mouth wouldn't open properly anymore. He glanced to the side, to where Felicita should be. But she wasn't there.—'It's true,' he said, reflecting. He turned laboriously onto his left side, towards the wall. The bed creaked. He drew his arm under the blanket, because he was getting really cold. He smacked his lips, as they were very dry.

Then he looked between the wall and his bed. There it was already properly dark. There was a line of dust on the edge of the side plank of his bed, and it was almost white. He felt comfortable now. One knee rested heavily on the other. —'Treze should give me some fresh milk,' he thought. 'It's going to be too late to come soon, silly woman.' He thought he heard the handle of the back door. He waited for a while with his ears pricked.—'It probably wasn't her,' he said under his breath, and listened for a little longer, till it made him feel tired in his chest. Then he thought: 'It probably wasn't anyone.' Then he heard, under the window, something rummaging around like a snout in tough grass. 'It'll be her with her goat,' he reassured himself this time. But no one came in. —'I'm lying here all on my own,' he thought.

He let his head roll to the other side, and adjusted his limbs, painfully. It was clearer to him now, but it was completely dark. His bed was bright yellow in the dark. And he also saw his cap hanging from the chair. Yes, it was his cap. But he didn't care. His head was so hollow inside, and so big. What did he suddenly think of? He couldn't remember, but his lips were sticking together.—'How alone I am lying here!' he sighed. He was rather angry, as he used to be at his wife.

—'How long has she been gone?' he wondered, and he began counting. But he couldn't manage it. 'It's already too dark,' he soothed himself. He closed his eyes and saw a great, circular space in which nothing was visible but a double yellow swarming. He wanted to go on thinking. But he couldn't anymore.—'I'll just have a nap,' he said to himself, and he settled down properly to sleep. He lay deep and close and no longer felt what he was lying in. The swarming darkness in his eyes turned blue and there were yellow and green balls rolling around in it. His head became warm. He moved his tongue against his gums, and it was no longer as dry. And his thick knees were warm too, and his belly. 'But I still shan't be able to sleep,' he said to himself again and it was as if he found it necessary to feel unhappy. 'I'm lying here far too alone.' And then he thought: 'And I've been alone for so long' . . . He had no pain now, and was nice and warm everywhere, but it was as if he was about to burst into tears. There was no resistance, but something like stubbornness, because he was lying there alone, all alone. He used to be angry when he came home from work and saw his whole litter of children. Now he felt his sick loneliness. Again, it suddenly occurred to him that he was dying. And a whining voice in him said:

'I'll never get what I want.'

He opened his eyes a little, but it was as if he did not open them: the same blue darkness, and the velvet balls. Again, he closed his eyes, which were already tired from having been opened a little. His eyes were now warm too and even his chest. He could no longer feel himself lying there. Where on earth was he? There was his wife again. No, it was Bertha, the eldest. She had once had a little white dog with curls. The balls in the darkness, they rolled about like dogs with white curls . . . But again, there was a weeping voice within: 'I'll never get what I want.'

Now that darkness became white, like milk is when it grows dark. No, that wasn't it: his head was now white as milk, inside. Then there came like a distant tune: 'I'll . . . never . . . get . . .'—But that white, that round white, which did not shine, began to move gently. 'I'll . . . never . . . get . . . what I want': it was as if they were singing to lull him to sleep—'I expect it's Bertha.' and he saw someone standing there in the swaying motion, in a blue apron amid that white. 'But I still won't be able to sleep. I've never got what I wanted. I'm . . .'

Then he saw very clearly that it wasn't his daughter Bertha.

It was a young girl with a blue apron. She had lovely blonde hair, which was smooth and brown from the butter; she had a pure face that shone like an apple, and pale blue eyes like a calf's. And she was very neatly dressed in a cotton jacket and an apron, which, just unfolded, lay in a waffle pattern across her belly. It was as if her hands came from the washtub. She did not smell of anything. She looked as bright as spring after a fresh morning shower.

'Bah, bah, Nand, you've never got what you want,' she said. Her mouth was moist and red: 'O—Bah!' And her mouth remained a little open and her eyes laughed.

'Has she come here to make fun of me?' thought Nand grumpily. And he thought he said it to her, but he didn't.

'Bah,' said the girl again, as if she had not heard him. And then she was silent for a little. But then she no longer smiled and said:

'Nand, don't you recognise me. I'm your Eyes. Still, I've always been with you since I'm your Eyes. But you're growing old, man, and that's why you've forgotten me. And that's why you say that you've never got what you wanted, Nand. —Nand, don't you remember then? You were only a peasant farmer, a cowherd with one animal, and for the last five years you've had no animals any longer, because you sit by the fire with your pipe and have no land anymore. But you were always a good farmer. During the week you didn't see much else except your workplace and your bowl of food, and you had to think about what needed to be done. But on Sundays after mass you didn't go off playing skittles in the skittle alleys like the others and drinking a drop of gin at the game; but you went round your land and enjoyed it. You saw the sky, and if it was blue you were glad, if it hadn't been dry for too long. But if the drought had gone on for too long then you were glad if the sky promised a downpour of rain. You saw that on Sunday, for during the week one works. It is on Sundays that you saw the damage the hail had caused in the orchard; but a wise peasant sells his fruit while it's still in blossom, and so you weren't that bothered. Archangels in the sky are signs of a storm; but if the grain is not too high, it can withstand it. On the contrary, it's good for it . . .

'But it is mainly your land that you saw, on Sundays. It lay round and high, but that is good for drainage. In the early spring you can still see the earth between the sprouts of grain; but in May the limp ear forms and you are content. The rape-seed blooms and is so yellow it hurts your eyes;

and at night the fruit trees are even whiter than
during the day, with all their blossoms. But it's sad
when you see the tops of the potatoes burnt black
from the frost, at that time; but it is still early in
the season and they can still put out new shoots
. . . When the summer comes, it is something else
again that you see. On Sunday mornings you go
walking among your patches of grain. You see that
the rye is yellow as a dandelion; but the wheat, a
little later, is as red as beer. The green of the clover
is very green, but its fat bunches are already as
beautiful as roses. The potatoes are also in flower,
white or like the mallows that grow in wet corners. At that time you see the water too, because
it is flat, and shiny. Because it is the time when
nothing can hide from the sun. It is the time of
the sunflowers by the dung heap, and by the back
door the dahlias as big as children's heads . . .
When autumn comes you dig up the potatoes;
on Sunday after vespers, the cowherds come in
their first-communion clothes, and make fires of
the tops for roasting spuds in. The smoke lies in
long wisps across the land. You see that getting
on towards evening, when you go for a game of
cards . . . Afterwards it is ploughed up, and on
Sundays you see the work of the shire horse, and
the earth that lies turned in fat, purple scales.

Then you sowed with your sowing apron on, with a wise grasp and wide sweep, and the firm tread of someone sowing his own land. You even did it on Sunday, because one must take the time as it comes, and the work one enjoys doing.

'If the beets are being got in, then winter is at the door. You've seen it often enough, the trees turned black with the wet, and the crows sailing through the air, and looking for carrion on the empty land. And then it's snow, great broad tracts of snow on the earth and on the roofs. A farmer has no work then except for a little in the house and the barn. But through the window you see the snow under the leaden sky, the white snow that immediately turns blue . . .

'And Nand, you have seen so many other things. You have seen the town and lots of inns, when you went to market to sell your calves with their long legs and the bare round spot on their foreheads like a sacred host. You always had those small Breton cows, and you can still see them in your shed, or when your children led them along the canal. Once you bought a dog for pulling carts. It was a massive beast, yellow like the butchers had. On the way home, it tugged at the lead so hard that you had to trot the whole time. You saw then, that summer afternoon, how the dust can rise when you walk. All the leaves were wiggling on the willows along the road. And you couldn't even pop into the *Half Way Inn* to grab a crafty pint, that dog was pulling so hard . . . —Do you remember, in the town you saw two posh houses where your daughters were in service. One can relax in the kitchen. And you also saw the Brussels Exhibition, and you still remember very well how it made your head spin and your legs hurt with the effort . . .

'And then, have you forgotten, Nand? Didn't you have your wife, your Wanne? You were not long out of the army. Your father was still alive. One morning in spring you saw her passing by. There happened to be a fresh wind blowing. All her hair blew onto her forehead, because she had lots of those fine ringlets. On her body and legs the wind made her clothes blow backwards. She was laughing too; she was red as a cabbage. You immediately started to fall in love with her. You married her. She gave you children, like peonies. And she was certainly always a good wife . . . Bah, Nand, did you never get what you wanted? Are you forgetting Wanne your wife? And what about the children then? You saw them all grow up. They were like flowers, like peonies. They were good children, and they worked for their parents.

Domien got married a little too early, but still he's
dutiful. He's in America. You've not seen his children. But you know all Bertha's children. She's a
good woman, and she does her duty by her twelve
children. You know, don't you, that the eldest is
called Nandje? . . .'

The young woman said nothing after this
question. And Nand said to himself that he knew
about Nandje. He was just like Bertha when she
was small, but he was a boy. He smiled. Bertha
was still concerned about him, bringing eggs for
him every week. She had lots of chickens. Her
husband fiddled about with the chicken run on
Sundays. In the week he worked in town. You
earn a lot more with that than with farming. He
was a good man. But Bertha was good too. Was
that Bertha standing beside him now, or was it
Nandje? Yes, he had had no complaints about his
children. Or about his wife, not by a long chalk.
A person shouldn't brag, but he had always done
pretty well, with the animals and with the land.
It's just . . . It's just that a person is never . . .
Isn't that so, Bertha, you know, don't you, child?
Bertha? Isn't that so, Bertha? . . . Bertha, why don't
you answer me? Bertha . . .

He wanted to turn over a bit. But he didn't
have to. He saw without turning over. It wasn't

Bertha. Nor was it the girl with the fresh apron. But another woman was standing there now.

'It's true, man, it's true . . .'

And she opened and closed her eyes elegantly. Her face was very white, but you couldn't see what it looked like. But that didn't matter. She was dressed completely in black, like Marie Burgemeesters when she sits behind the curtain in the cool front room in the afternoons with her needlework. You don't see her sitting there unless you know. She's no longer young, but has perfect manners. One could not see this one here very well either, with her dress without an apron. But one could hear her speak in a deep voice, like the organ in church when it plays quietly with a kind of trill.

'It's true, man,' she said; 'with the pleasure of his eyes alone a person won't make fat soup.'

She spoke daintily, like the tenant famers' daughters who've been to boarding school. She kept opening and closing her eyes: always a white spot and a dark spot, so that it began to tire Nand out. He closed his eyes too, and there was just the beautiful blue darkness. He had to laugh a bit at this. It was as if he had played a trick on that Marie Burgemeesters. 'Let her go on talking!' he thought . . . but he had to listen anyway, because what she said was sound, and as beautiful as a trembling organ during the consecration. And she said:

'With your eyes you would be nothing, if you had no ears: Nand, man, I'm your Ears. I always have been, although you didn't know. But I don't hold that against you, since you always used your hearing well. And it has given you pleasure, has it not?

'Think about it: whether old or young, you always lay awake for a long time listening for the cock to crow, the sign that you had to get up for work. And it was only on Monday morning, when your head was a bit heavy from the pints of beer, that you didn't lie and listen, and in the winter, when you didn't have to get up before dawn and the cockerel crowed in the middle of the night: then, already awake, you lay there for a bit and said: "Get lost!" but you heard the animals, which started getting restless in the shed, and you got up anyway, with gooseflesh on your calves from the cold, so that the hair stood on end . . . But in spring, when you lay waiting for the crowing of the cock, there was always a bird that kept you awake with its song. It's the bird that always has something to ask, one would say; or in rainy weather, the water bird that peeps like a pump. —Right, you're up. Now there are a hundred birds fighting and fussing in the trees, while the dew splashes down from them. Your wife's skirts wrap around her. While she makes coffee, you are already in the farmyard. The cow is trampling her straw; the goat is scratching itself on the wall of the shed; the pig's snout gives a wet snort under the half door. You go back to the house. Your wife stands in the doorway and calls: "Tee! Ti-ti-ti-ti," and all the hens trip over themselves in their cackling rush, while the stately cock that lifts his legs high, gives a suspicious "Cock, cock, cock." And you hear all that, and you enjoy everything going so well. In the summer everyone has left for work at that time. From flax harvesting time till after the oat harvest you have to be up early. And on the road you hear the echoing procession of the workmen, while it is still dark in the houses. Every so often they stop and there is a long, beautiful call, on their way, to upbraid their mates who have not come out yet. And where they walk on the paths, the flax rustles, or they make the grain rustle and shake it loudly with their hands. And in no time at all there is the singing fall of the pickaxe; you hear the whetstone shimmer over the steel, and from afar the jolly hammer sounds. In autumn weather, it is later in the morning that the rain patters against your window. You're not in such a hurry, although the cock crowed a while ago.—"The cock will soon grow hoarse from this weather," you think, and you pull your trousers on. You stay in the house a bit later now, and you lounge about. Now you hear the noises inside the house better: the children gabbling or shouting before they go to school; your wife washing up in the sloshing water. She tells you something. Then you go and thresh in your barn, and the flail thuds in time with a glad force. Or you need to winnow, or to sieve with the sieve that hangs from the loft; and then you hear the grains falling like hail on to the tarpaulin. In the stall next door the pig snores and sighs. On the manger sit the pigeons behind their screen, stamping their feet and cooing. —And isn't it true, in the winter the morning has no sound, and you can't hear the snow . . .

'But at midday!—When, in May, you come home at midday: hark how your wife sings as she strikes the churning pole. Not much is said at table, because you're eating. But it's May, and so children come, or old duffers and they carry the Maypole with the paper flowers and the basket of eggs, and they sing *Jesus the lovely Maypole*. They come at noon, because the farmer is at home too then. And then the song is over, then they are given their two eggs. After the meal it's time for relaxing. But it's only when the hay has been piled up, that leisure time comes. You lie on your belly in the cold grass; on your belly because of the bumblebees. They buzz around your ear till it hurts. At first you can't sleep, but in the end they buzz you to sleep. And then you don't hear the snoring of the others anymore, who are lying there in the orchard, but you yourself snore so loud, that you start awake.—Do you remember? In the approaching autumn you hear, while you're eating your lunch, the apples falling with a sweet thud out of the silent tree into the lush grass. A little later, the children start hitting with pitchforks or poking with long bean poles in the walnut tree, so that the thick foliage rustles loudly and the nuts tumble down like marbles. And it will become the time when, while you are eating in the cowshed the cow will start lowing for food. Because the animals will be inside now, because of the wet, and because winter is coming on. And in winter when you come home, at midday, it is not your wife that you hear singing in the distance: it is the Christmas pig squealing and choking under the slaughterer's big knife. You are quickly there: you hear the hair being singed off; you hear the hard scrubbing-brush over the skin; you hear the plentiful splashing of water. Once the opened-up animal is hanging on the ladder, you can go to eat, and tomorrow, Sunday, there will be chops.

'And as it gets towards evening . . . —Do you remember, do you remember, Nand, what it's like, when it's gradually getting towards summer, and you can sit at the door for a bit with your pipe? Evarist was already courting your Bertha. You liked him. He was a bricklayer's mate, in town, he didn't drink. Drink wrecks everything; a drop of gin after High Mass on Sundays, and in the evening a couple of pints playing cards. When you're still young it's a bit different, then it's every-one's right to be drunk on occasion; but you must be able to leave it alone in time. Evarist didn't drink. In the evening he came from town, from a distance white with lime dust, on his bike that rat-tled gently closer. Then he would go and squat for a bit against an apple tree. Bertha was knitting by the doorway so that the needles clashed together. They chatted very sweetly. The sky whispered. Bertha laughed, so that it was like a glow. And the cows came back from the meadow, quietly low-ing . . . You crept into the pig sty. Wanne, your wife was already there; she had already heard the sow squeaking, sighing and whining. You turned on the globe lamps: the sow was not yet giving birth. But you stayed with Wanne and you even played a game of cards whispering there in the straw. Then the sow, lying on her back, with her closed eyes from which water ran, groaned a little louder and, suddenly gave a loud "oh!"; it was the first piglet. After that everything went smoothly; she gave a few more short squeals; she stamped with her front feet and made the straw crackle; then she just rolled about a bit and snuffled her young ones with her wet snout. She had fourteen. Wanne stayed with her for a bit to make sure she didn't have a turn. You went outside. The whole heavens were singing loudly with the song of a nightingale, to which you would listen all your life . . . —But it is especially in late summer that the evening is loud. All the ponds of the chateau are croaking with frogs; it is as if those creatures like living with rich people. With the poor it's the cricket, the clattering cricket who does not live far from his winter lodgings. But it is the flax-harvesters who in the evening distance ring out most beautifully, when a section is finished and they sing happily on their work in the moonlight, and together they answer the question "Shall we eat the harvest porridge?" with a long, high-pitched "Yes!" in the affirmative to the skies. At St John the children crow like young cocks. And later, all the grain is picked: when the folk come in from the fields, all the red evening sun on the glistening sweat of their bare chests, then you hear them coming on their rough clogs and their singing blares out: "And there's still oil in it, oil in it!" . . . Now all the mosquitoes swarm, the mosquitoes are razor sharp. It is a sign that the evening is soon going to be quiet.

'But in autumn it is not quiet. You are indoors, in the approaching darkness, and the harsh wind blows under the door up against your trouser legs. You hear it swirling in the chimney and shaking the cowshed doors. It can yell like a woman in labour, and rage like the village policeman when he's drunk. And he is quite often drunk! . . . And the children listen. But they are content to play school. You hear that they have to say "Sister" to Bertha. You hear that Bertha beats in time on the back door, at which the others say: "Ba, be, bi, bo, bu" But you hear your wife say: "I'll light the lamp: then we won't hear the wind so much." So, winter comes into the land, sad because you always hear it raining so. I know, it can do no harm, and everything is harvested, but if you have to go to the animals, which are restless because their evening feed, you have to put a jute sack on top of your waistcoat, and you hear your clogs squelching along. But the beautiful time of song from Christmas Eve to Twelfth Night! "O star, O star, whither shall we go?"; and when the carol was over, it was suddenly very quiet. And "We three kings of Orient are" . . . I can see from your mouth, Nand: it's as if you were there . . .

'Because isn't it true, Nand, think about it: you enjoyed all that. I know full well you weren't a great farmer, but a man is a man, and has pleasure from his ears. You may not have been much more than a cowherd, but . . . !

'Isn't that foolish woman going to stop soon?' it began going round in Nand's head. 'With all her words in my ears it's as if a spider were running round in my head. It's as if I had nothing but my ears. Isn't it just as if I . . . ?'—It now went on and on, like a bobbin, a bobbin that plays across the loom. 'Isn't it as if a person can do nothing else . . .' It turned into a jumble of the same repeated words in his tired head, constantly confused. He tried to put them in order. He wanted to say it carefully with his own lips. He could no longer hear that Marie Burgemeesters. He had to say with concentration: 'Just as if I blooming well can't do anything but . . .'

Then he was suddenly startled by a loud laugh.

BUT his fright was just as quickly dissolved in
a kind of clarity. He did not need to open his
eyes to see very clearly.—'It's easy,' he thought. But
what he saw made him irritable again. Wasn't that
that little slag from the edge of the wood?—He
had already forgotten that Marie Burgemeesters.
But now, lying half over him was the blowsy
daughter of the shoemaker from the edge of the
wood, who also carves clogs from green wood,
and in winter makes Lord Jesuses on the cross in
pharmacy bottles. But you have to take him those
bottles yourself.—In his black hovel that clings
like a snail's shell to the hilly side of the wood,
it smells of mouldy pitch and wet, trampled autumn leaves. 'Yes, but,' Nand thought now, 'that
chap must be long dead!' He had been with his
slut of a daughter in the wood, in the evening.

But, he could say: he was still young at the time; he did not have to account to anyone. And now he had to laugh about it . . . Where could she be now, filthy Zulma from the edge of the wood? But she was lying half over him, her clothes full of dirt that had clung to her body, two dry leaves in her dusty flaxen hair, her two hands on either side of his hot head, which were red as meat. Her skirts smelled of pitch and wet woodland earth and the innards of wild rabbits. And that rose into Nand's nose, so that he wanted to say: 'You can smell it's you! Little slut!'

But he couldn't say it. For she sat upright, and he saw the full clarity of her face and the brightness around her face, which was cunning; and she laughed again like a turkey, and answered:

'Ha, there's no chance of that, Nand, of you're not being able to smell. Aren't I your Nose then? Yes, Nand, my lad, I'm your Nose. Ha! We've done dirty things in our lives! And you can't say we didn't enjoy them.' She laughed again, but more quietly and as if to herself. She said: 'It began, Nand, when you were still a toddler.' Nand had to laugh.—'It's true.' Although he didn't really know what was true. But he listened with pleasure to that crazy Zulma as she told her story:

'You remember: it started in the kennel. You can't have been anymore than three years old. The dog had puppies, and you wanted to see. The dog was away with your father, pouring liquid manure into a barrel. You crawled into the kennel and you still remember how it smelt, hot and deathlike like piled-up ox hides in the barns of big farmers, and also sour as old milk. You didn't know that at the time, but you smelt it and now you know. You did not see the puppies: but you sat in that warm, dark kennel, on the bitch's short dusty straw, which smelled pungently. You liked it there, and lay down for a while. Then there was a squirming about in the kennel and there was something that grabbed you softly by your nose and started sucking on it. It was the young puppies. You were frightened; you crawled out. The puppies, dragging on their bellies, followed you. They stopped at the entrance to the kennel, on their fat sides, eyes closed, mouths gasping for air.

'You remember, from when you were small, the smell of the hot bread, when your mother let you sit in the bake house; and the apples in the upstairs room, which you cannot reach because they are on the wardrobe; and the powerful breath of your father, who chewed tobacco, when on

Sundays, after a gin or two, he ran his rough chin over yours for fun.

'From the time when you went to school, you remember the teacher's hair. He had a white pasty face, but on Sunday he used to put pomade in his hair. He led the children to High Mass. In church you sat beside him. You saw his hair, all shiny. It smelled of roses and vinegar. You can still smell the wash tub of Fientje, the town clerk's servant, when the master told you to take the message that he would come to play cards that evening. There was a corner of the churchyard; it was the time of your first communion; and in that corner you always gathered with your mates, to whisper and intrigue; there was a thick patch of dandelions which in the evenings stank like cat's piss.

'And do you remember, Nand? We took our first communion together. You always sat look-ing at me during the lesson, as if you were angry with me. You once hit my skirts with your clog. The priest smelt of snuff and the church of warm butter-milk and candles. Then we didn't see each other for four years. But one evening we met by the edge of the wood. We went into the woods. The woods smelled of turpentine, for cleaning the stoves. We lay down. The ferns smelled of pepper. At least a thousand creatures were running around on the ground, and they smelled of cockchafers, when you smell them properly. And Nand, you smelled like cheese . . . When you returned to the farmer, where you were a cowherd, you went straight to your bed, in the cowshed, without saying good-night. Your head was light and your heart was wandering. The cows smelt clumsy. You thought of me, and you couldn't tell what I smelt of.

'And then you courted Wanne, Nand. You had aimed a little above your station, but you'd just come back from the army and you weren't bad looking. In the evenings you went a-wooing, with your waistcoat on. In the spring you went past the ploughed-up sections; there the barrel of manure stood waiting for the following day, smelling like blackcurrant.

'A little later in the year it was the lime trees that smelt sour and sweet; on every poor house there was an elder bush which seems to breathe; there was in addition to all that, the hay that smells like a pipe of good tobacco from town. Wanne's mother boiled the cooking pot, where the potato peel has the same smell all year round. And Wanne smelt of nothing but cream. But when there was a fair on, and the whole village smelt of waffles and warm beer and festive chops, you went dancing with her in the tent, and then the smell of Wanne's sweet sweat intoxicated you.

'You got married and so time passes, man. You had to toil hard . . . You hung your head in the glowing corn, wielding the pickaxe powerfully, and your burning head smelt like a huge rye loaf. Then you straightened your back in the air, to have a drink, and the cool water flowed through your mouth like mint. The drunken bumblebees bumped into your naked shining chest, and they smelt of all kinds of things and it was like warm rye bread too.—If you came home late at night, you ate the potatoes with onion sauce. Onion sauce smells of onion sauce, which should be much sourer. You took your youngest on your lap, it smelled like butter cloths. The rest smelt of sour apples, of the dung heap or the dovecote, depending on where they had been playing. As they grew up your Triphon was there. It never worked properly. When he was fifteen, all he dreamt of was a bike. He was apprenticed to the smith. He smelt of linseed oil and axle grease. But Bertha had always smelt freshly of soap . . . Then you went and sat outside for a bit, Nand. You sat among the lilies, and they started to smell of your pipe; but your pipe also started to smell a bit of the lilies. And when the children had gone to bed and Wanne was ready for bed, and her arms still smelled of the washing-up. And her jacket always smelt of yeast: then you dawdled a bit about going to bed with her. But you got up and got your dragnet out of the shed and put your cap on. You sat in your flat-bottomed boat that is moored on the River Leie. You cast your net and waited. The water was smoky. Above it there was a little breeze that smelt of the cold trees from the orchards across the Leie. But in the boat, so close to the water it smelt of soggy, muddy decay which immediately sticks to your skin. And you mustn't sit there for too long on the water, as it gives a man a headache, from all the sodden stuff you bring up with the net that smells of mud. And what do you catch? A few elvers; a gudgeon now and then; and occasionally there is a perch among them, then you hear it splashing about in the water before the net is completely up . . .

'And so a person grows old, Nand, my man. The children were grown up and you didn't want to go too far from your farm anymore. And that's why you couldn't sleep so well anymore, at night, in the time of toil. And the mosquitoes came and stung you, didn't they? But you rubbed your face and hands with paraffin, and that kept them off you; but then it was Wanne who kept you awake, because the stench woke her up and she grumbled.—Or in the winter you got into bed with you manure-spreading jacket on, for the warmth, because as the years go by a person feels the cold more, but then she snored again because it stank. As if you had ever played up because she could sweat so much at night, so that the whole bed smelt of it. But you said nothing; you just shifted away a bit . . .'

And Zulma laughed again, to herself. But Nand was no longer thinking of Zulma. He was thinking of Wanne. Wanne had died. He still remembers very well: she smelt strangely of wax. No: of the dry, paper nest of mice he had once found on the manger. No: she smelt, she smelt of . . .

'Leave me in peace!' there was a motion of resistance in Nand. 'Always about smelling of this and smelling of that! Always just smell and no taste!'

'What do you dare say there?' came a sudden unyielding reproach.

NAND was not startled by this: she was like that, she was always like that, Boldina the priest's maid. Because it was Boldina the priest's maid: no need to ask. Apart from that, Nand was lying too comfortably now to be surprised about anything. He was lying very still, deep and warm. He felt blissful. Shouldn't he say hello to Boldina? But no: since he was asleep. No, he wasn't asleep. But she must think he was asleep; isn't that so when a person is ill . . . Was he really ill then? He scarcely knew anymore. But yes, he was ill; in fact, he was dying, and she was bringing him something from the priest to eat. Should he open his eyes? It was a long time before he could imagine that it might be a good idea to open his eyes. Meanwhile she was standing there next to him. He knew. He didn't have to see her. She was wearing her jacket with fringes. There was also snuff in the folds of the flat bow of her beaded cap. She again had red patches on her severe face, today. She always had a medicine bottle of gin in her pocket: everyone knew. She said:

'You've never turned your nose up at a drop or two, Nand.'

But Nand didn't move or contradict her. He mustn't show that he wasn't asleep. If she had something to eat with her, she would say so. He did have the taste of hot pancakes in his mouth, with apples, but that doesn't matter. She mustn't know. Yes, a drop of gin, that can do no harm. In the winter it warms and in the summer it dries your sweat. But you mustn't drink too many . . . —'It's just as if I had drunk a drop of gin,' thought Nand now, as he was sweating a little inside, and needed to gasp for air . . .

'You're right,' said Boldina, a person needs to exercise their senses. It prickles the tongue, and it does you good. I'm sure you know that, Nand? I'm your Taste. A drop from time to time, a pipe of tobacco, and around Christmas Day, when you go to pay your rent, a cigar from the baron . . .'

Nand agreed: 'Yes, yes, those are good things. He savoured the taste, but with a mouth that was too dry. His opinion was: 'When it comes to eating

and drinking there are many things that are good.'
And his mouth became a little wetter thanks to a
tiny bit of spittle. He had to swallow. It was quite
difficult and brought him back to the pain in his
knees. But that lasted only a very short time: he
sank back into his blissful feeling. Because there
was the sound of a voice; he wasn't sure if it was
Boldina, the priest's maid, or the priest himself.
He couldn't care less. The voice said:

'Yes, there are many good things to eat and
drink. On Monday you get up and you have a
taste in your mouth that is bad: of wood or cop-
per, whichever you like. But you have coffee, hot
coffee, and that flushes you out. Coffee is always
good, even if you've swallowed your plug of tobacco by accident, and it tastes best on Mondays.
You drink it with your sandwiches, though you
haven't much appetite, on Mondays. That's why
a slice of fat meat is good on that day, at midday,
and tastes salty with your potatoes. The potatoes
mustn't be too fluffy: if they're like eggs they'll
almost taste like eggs, won't they? And if you're
not working in the winter and get nothing but
potatoes at midday, they should be good, but they
become bad. But you have your porridge and
that's always good; it's easy. And in the evening
you have your potatoes with some salad cut up

among them and the sour sauce with crackling. The whole village smells of it, in the evening, and even if you hadn't worked until you were tired, the smell alone would be enough to make you hungry.

'On Tuesday it's almost the same. But you may have no bacon at midday. But instead you have, according to the season, French beans, mash with cabbage, or occasionally red cabbage. The rich eat salad without sour sauce; but you've got to be crazy to like that. Salad is insipid food. Peas, yes, are better, but the best ones go to town, for the rich, and a farmer has to be content with the fat ones. But red cabbage is best; it's sour, and you feel it in your stomach for a long time.

'On Wednesday, oh well, that's the same again, isn't it?; and Thursday too. But you eat the occasional apple too. The strawberries go to market. Blackcurrants and gooseberries are stuff for children. And all the other fruit is sold on the tree, and the fruit of the elder bush to the priest; Boldina makes syrup from it for his cough. But of course, a person has an apple. At noon an apple bee flies around every apple on the tree at lightning speed. And in the evening the trees are cloaked in dancing gnats. And they are nice and sour, good for thirst.

'Friday is market day. You go to town. You drink a cool drop; that is not abuse, provided you only drink two. And you also drink a half of beer. At midday you eat milk porridge with lumps in it, and you are given an egg with your potatoes. And for the rest of the day you are no good for anything. And in the evening you eat a fresh herring, which is salty.

'On Saturday morning the bread is as dry as bark. Now you can tell better that it tastes of bran. But on Saturday evening you eat the fresh bread, which turns the whole house upside down with its smell. And it sits nicely in the stomach like a waffle and occasionally repeats on you.

'And so Sunday comes. There are some who grab a drop of gin before High Mass. But you've never done that; you waited until after High Mass, because you were in the priest's good books. The others are from the other clique and they stayed at the back of the church. But you are at the front, and you wait until the town clerk has left, before leaving. And then you go, don't you, to drink a gin in *The Font*, no more than one at a time, unless you have a worm in your stomach: then you drink a drop of rhubarb which is as bitter as beer, which you have to taste before you buy it. But it is good for the worm and for everything.

—You have never been a great lover of skittles. And cards on Sunday morning are not on. They all remain standing and you can't sit comfortably and concentrate on your cards. So, what do you do? Ha, you drink another drop. And then you go round your land, and you see the big farmers going round their land with a spade; and they stand straight, but the poor farmers are all bent over with working.—But the air is already full with roast meat. You go home; it is Sunday; we sometimes eat soup, leek or something; but that is good for the womenfolk. We eat our own meat, from the tub; we've already slaughtered a goat, or it might be the cow that was coming down with the fever. It's a loss, but the rich people will buy a piece each, and in that way it will bring some money in. But anyway, you prefer pork . . . —You lie down in your bed for a bit, because Sunday afternoon is so long. When you get up you take a tour of your barns in your white shirtsleeves, and you smoke a good pipe. But you think that in a while you're going to have some ham. The ham has sat for a good time in the salt tub, drizzled with some lemon verbena and some fennel; then it dried for a time and it has been smoked; now it's hanging in the chimney breast, and there is no better food . . .

'So, the afternoon passes. Towards evening, you go past your land to the *Forest Hut* to play cards. You drink pints during the game. Before you leave you drink a nightcap. And you know full well that tomorrow you won't have any appetite. But what are you going to do about it? . . . That's the way of the world.

'But it's at fair time that there is the most eating and drinking! On Saturday it already smells of flans, the white ones with cream and the brown ones with gingerbread. When you come from the land in the evening, the women pass you with apple tarts as big as cartwheels on the way to the baker. And on Sunday it's a stew of carrots and chops from the summer pig, and then rice pudding to fill the gaps, and to finish off with a sandwich, because without that a person hasn't eaten. All afternoon it's a treat of waffles and flans and tarts for the women. The men start drinking lots of pints, and when they can't drink anymore beer, they have a gin and after the gin they have a glass of Leuven liqueur, against the tension in the bladder. And in the evening it's ham—you can't eat anymore. And towards bedtime you've eaten and drunk so much, that you don't know how you don't burst. And on Monday you're still wearing your white shirt; in the afternoon it's coffee with sugar balls, gingerbread and a half a slice of sweet-meat. And you join in, because the day before you were properly drunk. But in the evening you're still going to have a drop to drink, because you're thirsty. And you play a game of cards, and you win a pint of Oudenaarde beer . . .'

Nand knew all that and he felt warm and happy. As he lay there without moving, he was gently moved at the thought: 'Yes, I had that; thank God I had all that.' And his thoughts went further, and as they did he was more and more moved. He thought of the round baptism parties and the godmother who gradually became drunk from the halves of aniseed, mint and rum punch; he thought of the white first communion when one first drinks chocolate milk and then a gin, and he thought that Bertha, his beloved Bertha, had such beautiful stiff curls. At weddings the eating and drinking is even more excessive than at the fair, but each time it's a loss; one child goes here, the other there. Wasn't his Domien in America? And they left their old father alone with the burden of the land and the animals . . . —Nand almost cried at it. His gullet filled with warm water, from the dark recesses inside him; there was heat in his nose and in his eyes. God, they had all left him alone . . . And when he thought of the funeral meal for

Wanne, for his Wanne; and how he was suddenly completely alone, utterly alone; and that now he himself . . . Because yes, he was dying now, wasn't he? He was lying here; he was lying here so utterly deserted and alone . . . He lay there.

Then, then . . .

BUT he did not cry. A large dark figure was bending over him, a figure in all the folds of her hooded cloak. With thin fingers that trembled and made his blanket tremble, she tucked him in, plumped up his bedding, spoiled him, just like when he was a little boy and was occasionally ill. He was already consoled; not yet completely; but almost. He was comfortable. He was lying asleep. A warm breath weighed slightly on his eyelids and his own breathing adjusted to that breath. He lay deep, deep. He felt his head lying very deep in the pillows. His whole body lay under a soft pile of blankets, as it were. And he went into his head, as if he were sleeping a little . . .

—But he felt no resentment or regret at waking up again, when the figure, very warm and quiet, asked at his ear:

'Do you recognise me? Do you recognise me?

But he did not have to recognise her, because it was his mother . . .

She took the chair with the cap hanging on it. He thought as if in a deep distance: 'Surely mother will put my cap on the chest. But she had already put it there. She sat at his bedside: he could feel it. He could hear the little beads of her rosary. She started saying her rosary. He heard her mumbling the words in the dark. The dark was soft and warm as black velvet. She mumbled her rosary. He heard it. But it was as if, in the drowsiness into which he sank lower and lower, he heard:

'You're lying comfortably now, you're lying warm like that, now I've tucked you in, my boy. You are lying comfortably, aren't you? A poor man has only the warmth of his body to cure himself, and from cold comes death. But now you're lying there warm, my boy, and you can rest . . .

'Oh, how the poor suffer from the cold! Yes, when you're young the cold of the frost or wind stirs your blood, so that you know the pleasure of throwing out your arms and legs, so that you start scintillating with the glow to the tips of your fingers and toes. The children warm themselves up by laughing and throwing snowballs. And when the young girls feel the snowflakes that slowly come and settle on their cheeks, or even the merciless needles of the icicles, they giggle, because they are like chilly but hot kisses. But if they lie in bed and don't have a good blanket, they shiver with cold; the children cry with the cold; and it is only the cowherds and their mates, in the hard winter nights, that are warm enough to dream of love. For the poor man has no riches but his warmth. It is a blessing of the married state, that sleeping together you are warm. And nothing is sadder than the cold of widowers.

'But when you are warm you have courage. You're nice and warm now, aren't you, Nand? Then you can think of your young days when you could work up a sweat playing in the farmyard, or went with the harvesters and as you harvested, you felt deep in your body hotter than the sun itself. But then came the break, when you waded through the stream with your bare legs or poured the cold water from the jug into the cellars of your throat, then you were grateful to the heat for allowing you to refresh yourself. And when you married: aren't the close nights nice for married people? And when you grew old: don't you feel that it is only because of the warmth that you can still move and have your thoughts and can still speak? Because cold makes you brittle and hard as glass, in your head and in your legs.

'But now you're lying warm, Nand, in your good bed. There are no more calluses on your fingers from working. You can feel over your stomach the soft worn feeling of your cotton shirt, and where you are lying, the graininess of your good linen sheets on your thighs. And it's not much, the pleasure you get from this, but it is reassuring. You feel, on either side of your head, the reassuring caress of your woollen pillow. And if you feel a cooler caress over your forehead, it's good to combat the rarefied glowing in your head. Can you feel a bit of coolness on your forehead, Nand? Then you can still think of your children and your wife, then you can think of your whole life . . .'

And yes: Nand could still think of them; he could still think about them in the twilight of sweet sleep, in which he knew he was now lying. Because he knew he was no longer awake. Why should he still be awake?: it was good like this, like this . . . And it went on mumbling in him:

'Nand, the skin of a new-born infant is the softest thing to feel in the whole world. It is almost nothing more, you'd say, than a smell, than the smell of a flower or a biscuit. But when the children grow older, they bring you worries, when you feel that they are hot in the folds of their limbs. Because you know it means they are ill, Nand.—But you share the worries with your wife. You've known her a long time now, since you've had children who were sick together. You stand bent over their beds with her. Her arms are bare. When you went out courting her arms were cool and smooth as bobbins. Then with happy pride you felt your own arms, which were hard and full of knotty strength. And now you are standing here next to her, worried out of your mind. And you think of her hips which are broad, fat and warm and you felt almost ill the first time you put your hand on them . . .

'You weren't a big farmer, Nand, but you were a wise farmer. You polished the ploughshare with your own hand and felt the handle of the spade gradually become less scratchy. When your work was done, you were pleased with the roughness of your dog. The smooth hides of your cows filled you with contentment. And if you felt the heat of fever in the joints of the calves, you knew what to do, better than with your children.—You knew by sight alone, the grainy cold of tubs, the ribbed dryness of the butter churn, the icy malevolence of the scythes. Your wet hands on your corduroy trousers, Nand, and the scraping of your skin under the razor . . .

'So, you've grown old, Nand. You've felt the stiffness in your thick square knees. And you, Nand, you . . .'

Nand knew what he wanted to say. Look, he didn't know very well, because he was lying here so blissfully deeply and well and warm, and because he didn't really dare to know. But he still knew what it was he still knew. It was like a tiny light, burning in him; and he could not blow, he could not breathe without it going out, dying, disappearing, and he would never see it again. It was, it was that last thing in him, that he wanted to hold onto; it was the last of him, the last thing in his life: it was—that he had closed the eyes of Wanne, his wife, when Wanne died, with his thumb and forefinger, and that he could still feel it in his thumb and forefinger . . .

And now Nand suddenly lay there full of sad anxiety, because he was afraid it was going to go out, vanish, that last memory, and that he was going to die with all the sadness of that loss. Ha, what would it have all been, all that he had been able to enjoy with eyes and ears, with smell and taste, and feeling with his hands and feeling with his heart, if he must go with the pain of having abandoned what stopped him from dying? . . .

AND NAND lay in the depths of that unhappiness, that now started thrashing about all through his body, that choked his throat, that stabbed his wrists and knees. He tried to move; he wanted to stop it happening; he wanted to say, say that . . . But he could no longer speak; he twisted his tongue that would no longer untie; he forcibly opened his eyes, as if he wanted to beg for help . . .

And look, he suddenly became very calm. He had opened his eyes. The room lay very clean in sweet evening brightness. He saw everything nicely in its place: the chest with the Virgin Mary on it; his old cap on the rush chair. And he saw something else: he saw Wanne, his old Wanne, standing full of compassion by his bed . . .

But it wasn't Wanne: it was his awakening soul . . . But it was Wanne, though . . .

And he saw that Wanne was smiling peacefully at him. One by one she slowly took her clothes off, which she folded neatly and put on the chair with his cap. She was going to come to bed too, he saw. And now he was certain that henceforth she would be with him forever . . . He saw that she knelt down to pray. He closed his eyes. In his head he prayed along with her: 'Our Father, which art in Heaven . . .'

And when he had finished, he waited for a moment. He waited for Wanne to say something. But she didn't say anything. Then he wanted to say something himself. What would he say, that . . . ? He waited a little longer. But then began smiling craftily. Now he knew what he had to say. He knew, oh, he knew . . .

And he opened his mouth, his black mouth. But he didn't say anything.

For he was dead.